THE LEGENDS
OF PRAGUE

The Legend
OF THE INFANT
OF PRAGUE

MEANDER

© Published by MEANDER Publishing, 2000
    Original title: The Legend of the Infant of Prague
© by Ivana Pecháčková
© Illustrations Jarmila Marešová

ISBN 80-902373-6-3

TABLE OF CONTENTS

The Story of Maria, Spanish Noblewoman 1555

A magnificent mare galloped along a path through fields bleached white and dry by the burning Spanish sun. Her sides shone with sweat, and her mane whipped wildly as the rider, bowed low over the horse's neck, constantly urged her on with his heels. The horse carried him as if he were no burden at all. In fact, his thin, boyish body seemed to have become one with the animal.

Suddenly, the horse swerved violently to the right, heading for the road to the palace. When a low branch knocked off the rider's hat, a long cascade of raven-colored hair tumbled down, blowing freely in the wind. The rider is a woman, a young girl, who is returning from a secret journey to the mountains. There she has just met with her cousin, Raul, for the very last time. He is the young man she had been growing up with, and to whom she had secretly hoped to be married. But instead, tomorrow she will journey as the bride of another strange man to his foreign land.

The slender rider was young princess Maria, the daughter of don Garcia Manrique de Lara who was one of the most powerful men in the land. He decided to promise her to a Czech nobleman Vratislav of Perstejn, who had asked the Spaniard for his daughter's hand in marriage. Now Maria must give up her home, her beloved Spain, and leave for a land in the north where the cruel winters seem endless and where the sun never shines enough. Moreover, she will hardly ever understand the strange language.

Echoes of the beating hooves of Maria's mare resounded in the vast courtyard of the palace. She passed right by the surprised grooms in front of the stables and headed towards the chapel. Only there could the unhappy girl seek her last comfort. In tears she sank onto the marble floor. She pressed her feverish face against the cool stone. „Lord," she whispered, „I beg of you, reveal what it is that you have in store for me. Why can't my life be happy like the lives of those whom I must leave? Why must I give up what is most dear to me? Without Spain I will wither like a flower without sun. If it is my fate to bear this cruel burden, I beseech you, do not leave me! Give me

strength, so that I might duly respect my husband and hold his homeland in the proper esteem!"

It was unusually cold in the chapel, and a faint light filtered through the stained glass saints, who watched gravely from the windows. The young girl was lost in prayer before the altar, her form cast in an otherworldly glow. One amber ray touched a tiny figure on the altar, bathing it in a clear light. Maria raised her head in surprise and stared at the illuminated face of the God's Son. His smiling eyes gazed down upon her with understanding. Peace and calmness washed over her heart. The love radiated by the Christ Child flooded her in powerful waves. She watched, amazed, as the Child moved its hand in a gesture of blessing and its mouth opened in a loving smile. „Do not despair, Maria," he said in a soothing voice. „You are destined to lead a good life."

The girl wiped away her tears and listened in amazement. „Tomorrow you will depart for the unknown, but do not fear, for you will soon grow accustomed to your new home. You will never cease to adore magnificent Prague at whose court you will reside. There, your husband will become a prominent diplomat, and you too will contribute to his success. You will not, however, ever forget your old home, Spain. Both you and your husband will provide her invaluable service more than once.

Maria listened to the tale of her life, and the apprehension in her eyes was replaced with wonder and relief. „Your task will be to spread piety and respect for me, the Infant Jesus. That is why your steps lead to Prague. I will guide you along all of your journeys – you will receive love and strength from me. I will always watch over your family, your Prague, the Kingdom of Bohemia… and the whole world."

It is said that the next morning, a splendidly equipped procession set out from Spain. They were carrying a beautiful bride to the Czech lands. The young lady went toward her new future with courage in her heart. To Prague, the bride carried with her the most precious gift of all… the statue of baby Jesus, the Infant of Prague.

The Story of Prague, A City Miraculously Saved

*T*he little Prague Child, which the young bride brought from Spain, soon became renowned in Prague. This occurred during one of the worst wars to ever afflict the Czech Lands. The cruelties lasted an entire thirty years. At that time, the Prague Child was not in the possession of a single family, but of the monastery of the Barefooted Carmelites in the Little Quarter of the city. Polyxena of Lobkowicz, the daughter of the Spanish noblewoman Maria, had decided to offer the miraculous statue to the order. She wanted the Holy Child, which had kept her family safe during the wars, to hold its protective hand over both the city and the country as well.

The fearful cry of battle, which spread throughout Europe in those times, made its way through the Kingdom of Bohemia into Prague. And, naturally, it was the dream of every foreign general to force that great city into submission.

In April of 1639, to the horror of the citizens of Prague, the watch towers again sounded the alarm. The powerful Swedish army, known for its cruelty, was besieging the city. They had been plundering the Czech Lands for years already, and everyone well knew what the invasion of Prague would mean – unbridled looting, murders, fires and sicknesses, misery and hunger…

When Jakub arrived home all out of breath with his horrible news, it was as if his mother had been struck by a terrible blow. The milk jug slipped from her hand and the fresh, warm milk – at that time extremely precious – quickly soaked into the earthen floor. Jakub's mother collapsed onto a stool, sank her face in her palms, and began crying bitterly. She was a widow; the war had taken her husband from her. She had to try very hard to feed the hungry mouths of her children. Just recently luck had smiled upon her, and she had managed to find a place in the Duke's kitchen. Finally her children's stomachs had stopped growling. And now such awful news! She could already hear the cries of drunken soldiers beneath the windows and the screams of innocent victims…

As someone pounded on the door, she jumped and clutched her frightened children to her, imagining the worst. Thank God it was only the baker's wife from next door.

„The Swedes are at the gates!" she gasped in horror. The neighbors fell into each other's arms. „It's the end – only a miracle could save us now. I will go to the Prague Child to pray for its help. I still thank him daily that he saved Betty from death's grasp. It's only a few months since her awful sickness, and the girl already has roses back in her cheeks. Oh! and we were planning her wedding for this fall," cried the baker. „Only God knows how we'll all end up!"

The widow comforted her neighbor, then threw a shawl over her shoulders, and they hurried off together for the Holy Infant. But the church was so full, that they could not fit inside. The frightened citizens of Prague had filled even the cathedral's front courtyard. Men, women, and children were bowed in prayer, humbly beseeching that their city and families be saved from harm.

Divine services were held day and night in the Church of Our Lady Victorious in the Little Quarter. The Swedes still had not invaded the city which was so defenseless, so temptingly offering itself in the spring sunshine; just reach out a hand and pick… They had set up camps beneath the gates and were watching at a menacingly close distance. Every night they sat by their enormous fires and sang rough soldier songs in which they already celebrated the rich and easy plunder. It was as if they meant to stay for eternity.

Early one morning, Jakub was carrying the dinner scraps home from the Duke's

kitchen, as he usually did. On his way from the Sternberg Palace, he stopped at the castle hill. From this point, he could see Prague as if it were on the palm of his hand. As was also usual, Jakub could never resist shooting a few stones at the Swedish encampment from his slingshot. He found a handy stone, pulled out his slingshot, aimed – and suddenly stood still with his mouth wide open. In the gray morning light, in the near dark, where the monitoring army's watch fires usually glowed, he saw only a few remaining soldiers, and even these soon disappeared over the hill.

The fearsome Swedish army had disappeared with the night. Jakub flew down the hill with this incredible news. How was it possible that the Swedes had left? How could they have given up such an easy war plunder?

The citizens of Prague found out what had happened from a prisoner who had managed to escape from the Swedish camp. It seems that the commander of the besieging army, General Banner, finally decided to invade the city that night. As soon as he issued the command, and the army prepared itself for the assault on Prague, a messenger riding a foaming horse dashed up to the general's tent. To everyone's great disbelief and disappointment, the army commander canceled his order after only a short discussion, and instead called for just the reverse – that the army instantly pull out.

How can we shed light on such an inexplicable twist of events? With some logical historical facts and arguments? Grateful residents of Prague have, for ages, ascribed this miracle to the Holy Infant. And thus was born the legend of the Prague Child, who is sympathetic to all, especially to those suffering from the greatest oppression.

The Story of Father Ildefons, General of the Carmelite Order 1737

*A*ship of no great size set out from the Sicilian port of Palermo, headed for Milazzo with a cargo of wheat and wine. The captain was an experienced sailor – as is every Sicilian, after all. He had waited until the last minute to decide whether to postpone the trip. The dark skies looked ominous. Finally, the port innkeeper had decided for him. He sent three passengers to his ship, which had been prepared for sailing since early that morning. They were monks, Carmelite brothers, and they were in great hurry. The oldest of them, Father Ildefons, the newly elected general of all Carmelites, and his companions were planning a visit to inspect a Carmelite monastery not far from Milazzo. Their pleading and some silver coins finally persuaded the captain. As soon as they were clear of the shore, the captain hoisted all sails, making the ship fly like an arrow in the strong wind.

„If there's some kind of storm brewing, we'll ride it out," the captain thought aloud. „If this wind holds, we'll be in Milazzo in no time at all."

Father Ildefons was the only one on deck who came from a landlocked country. He came from the very heart of Europe, from the Czech Lands, and had spent the majority of his life within the walls of a Carmelite monastery in Prague. The first time he had ever seen the sea was here in Italy. This splendid, endlessly changing natural wonder had bewitched him. Only on the shores of the sea had he found the calmness necessary for contemplation and prayer, a calm of which he had only dreamed amidst the turmoil of life in the city of Prague.

But now he nervously watched the storming wonder, his two Italian brothers, and the captain, who were restlessly watching the tossing waters below with ever increasing attention. It had never occurred to Father Ildefons that the sea could be so dangerous. The waves lifted themselves threateningly higher and higher, and one after another threw themselves against the boat, pushing it towards the dangerously close rocky coastline along which they sailed. Suddenly, the captain found that he had his hands full. He lowered first sail, then another one, again and again trying to steer the boat between the enormous waves and away from the dangerous shore…

The creaking poles and broken ropes indicated that the losing battle with the sea is hopeless. Soon the old Sicilian was at the end of his strength. „Father, I've lost control of the ship!" he tried to call above the roar of the waves. „Pray for our souls!"

Just then, an enormous wave lifted the ship like a feather and threw it against the jagged cliff, which had seemingly emerged from nowhere beneath the tumultuous waters. There was a ghastly crack of splintering timber which for a moment was even louder than the roaring of the waves. To their horror, another powerful wave rolled over the paralyzed survivors, threatening to carry off the wreck and either impale it upon a rock or send it to the depths below.

„Hold on tightly!" Father Ildefons felt the captain's arm lock around his shoulders. Then a giant wave swept over them and the water closed above…

When he opened his eyes, he thought he was in heaven. The sun was pleasantly warm, and he saw the faces of his brothers above him. And they were all alive and well! Father Ildefons lifted his head and looked out at the sea, which had finally begun to calm. Their destroyed boat had gone down in the depths, but the crew had managed to save themselves by clinging to the cliff. The captain, however, shook his head and pointed to the rising tide. The jutting cliffs were vanishing beneath it by the minute, and the water began to wet their feet.

„The sea won't give up its prize so easily," he said darkly. „Soon it will devour us too."

Father Ildefons clasped his hands to his chest and began to pray out loud. He suddenly felt the large book below his clerical robes, which he had put there for safety together with other important papers. It was an old and precious missal, ornamented with gold and silver. Father Ildefons hastily unwrapped the leather case with its significant contents. All the papers were destroyed by the salty water, but the book was unharmed. Its pages fluttered joyfully in the wind and opened themselves precisely to a picture of the Infant Jesus. It was the famed Infant of Prague, which Father Ildefons had cared for in Prague for years and to which he had directed his prayers, even in the instant when their boat had disappeared beneath the fiendish waters. His exhausted face lit up. He understood the miraculous preservation of the missal as a sign, and so he did not lose faith in their salvation, even though the water was rising quickly.

„A ship! I see a ship!" the captain suddenly cried in disbelief.

A large schooner, driven by the storm to this place where ships never sail, was making directly for the group of survivors. After their last minute rescue, Father Ildefons and his brothers sent their precious missal to the Infant of Prague as proof of their gratitude. This precious book had miraculously survived the shipwreck without harm. As miraculously as they themselves had. . .

The Story of Arsalan,
An Indian from the Peruvian Andes 1885

*T*he last part of the trail to the Indian village winds up mountain slopes above dizzying precipices and deep abysses, where dark waters roar threateningly below. Each time Pietro traveled in these awesome mountains, he couldn't help closing his

eyes at least a little. He was afraid of heights since childhood, and here, one misstep could cause them to plunge to the depths below. He had wandered with his fellow missionaries countless times along trails so narrow that even a horse couldn't find a foothold between the treacherous stones. There was no other choice but to close his eyes and entrust himself to God.

On this day, however, the young Italian missionary paid no attention to the ever-dangerous mountains. He was not thinking of the abysses, nor of avalanches nor even wild beasts of prey. In his mind, he was reliving the dramatic events of the previous days.

It was very difficult to overcome the pain in his heart caused by the loss of his friend and teacher Diego. The Indian had died in his arms just a few hours ago. Diego and his beautiful, wise sister Arsalan were Pietro's most devoted friends. They had been his first pupils in the New World, although the teacher had soon recognized that it was he who would, in fact, be the one to learn from his pupils. He knew so little about what life had been like in this remarkable continent before the arrival of white civilization. Diego and Arsalan had inspired him to plunge into the rich past of the Indians. They had told him of the wealthy and powerful empire of their forefathers and of the fame and tragic end of the Inca kings. What right had the colonists had to appropriate a foreign land? How could God have allowed this shameless exploitation of the Indians to occur under the pretext of spreading faith and education in His name?

Pietro had soon seen what the greed of the white colonists had done to the once proud Indians. They were forced to do only the worst forms of labor for the white settlers, laboring on plantations and in mines from sunrise to sunset often for only a handful of corn and just a few cocoa leaves.

„Your faith is good," Arsalan once said to him, „but it does not help my people. On the contrary, it adds to their oppression. If you truly wish to help us, you must do so in a different manner."

She then disclosed what the missionary had already begun to suspect – that Diego and the others were preparing for an armed rebellion. It was to be a mighty uprising, so that the whites would have to give the Indians back their freedom and return their stolen lands to them.

„You arrived here as a teacher to plant the seeds of evangelism among Indians," Arsalan had continued. „You must return home as a speaker for our evangelism. You must make people everywhere aware that Indians are not the backward slaves of white men, but proud warriors. And, if necessary, we will even use violence to take back our stolen lands. I am writing a book about this, so that the whole world will know the truth. And you will help me in the fight against the cruel oppression." Arsalan then embraced Pietro, for she was certain of which side he was on.

A couple of months later, the great Indian army rolled into Lima. Peru became a republic in which, as in old times, Indians would once again rule Indians. But the army of the Peruvian President finally managed to suppress and disperse the uprising. Diego fell in one of the massacres, while Arsalan and a handful of loyal followers fled to the mountains to hide themselves in a small village high in the Andes.

Last night Pietro received the news that Arsalan, exhausted from battle and the difficult march in the cruel cold, has come down with pneumonia and is in need of urgent medical attention.

Pietro had set out on his journey before dawn after gathering together the most necessary medicines. At a bend in the trail just below the Indian settlement, he caught sight of a tall man wading with difficulty through a field of snow. When the missionary caught up with him, he recognized the well-known Indian doctor.

The Indian greeted him gloomily, "I know how close Arsalan is to your heart, but she will not live past today's setting of the sun."

Pietro jumped off his exhausted horse and, in an eyeblink, ran the short distance to the hut the doctor pointed out to him. The girl's small body seemed to be lost in the pile of wool blankets. Arsalan didn't know about herself anymore and even stopped hallucinating. Her body was as cold as the icy snow of her native Andes Mountains, but she was still breathing. When he tried to lift her and press the medicine he had brought into her mouth, her body slipped without any resistance from his hand. He shuddered – he could sense the presence of death in the hut.

"Fight, Arsalan, do not give up! Now it is up to you to show your people the way! You must finish your book!" He shook her in despair.

"Arsalan is leaving us," said the calm voices around him.

He turned around and looked into the peaceful, reconciled faces of Arsalan's brothers and sank his face into his hands. He could not accept death with the same composure as these Indians.

He took the chain from his neck. He had received it as a gift from his mother and had worn it since childhood. A tiny figure was engraved on the decorated medallion that swung from the gold chain. The Prague Child. Pietro softly drew aside the girl's jet black hair and fastened the chain around her neck. He closed his eyes and began to pray silently. Gradually, the others around her bed joined him in his prayer.

They were already awaiting the dying girl's final breath when, suddenly, a deep moan rose from her breast. Then Arsalan began breathing more normally, and color

slowly returned to her pale cheeks. Finally, to the wonder and disbelief of Pietro and the Indians, she opened her eyes and smiled faintly.

„Deo gratias," whispered Pietro fervently. „Your endless love, Lord, knows no boundaries. It finds us everywhere. It even finds those who decide to go their own way…"

The Story of Little Elsa, The Baby From Cogoleto 1943

Barbara stamped her feet in the cold to warm up her stiff legs a bit. It was only November, but just then, around five in the morning, it seemed to her like it was already well below freezing.

The tired people were standing in silence for a long line for rationed war bread. Barbara jumped, startled, when a scrawny Siamese cat from behind the fence next to her screamed like a crying child. That scream reminded her of her own small baby, her one-month-old daughter Elsa, who slept at home alone in her cradle. It seemed like an eternity since she left the house, but the bread still hadn't come. "Elsa's surely sleeping," Barbara said to herself for the hundredth time. "She's warm, fed, and she's asleep, nothing can happen to her.".

„They're here!" called an older woman at the front of the line. The whirring of the motor could already be heard, but the car was still nowhere to be seen. The line of anxious people grew suddenly wary, „What's going on, for God's sake?"

The strange noise grew louder above their heads, and an ominous shadow spread over the dark sky. Then the square was shaken by a deafening explosion. The whole front facade of a house across the way caved in, and a cloud of dust filtered down onto the sidewalk.

„Air raid! American bombardment! Hurry, take cover!" came the distraught cries.

A small group scattered in panic across the square. The wails of the siren sounded all around, and a series of blinding flashes lit up the city.

„Mrs. Giusto! Hurry! Over here to the cellar!" The young woman felt someone drag her down the steps.

„I have a baby at home! I have to go get my daughter!" Barbara tried in vain to pull away. „She's home all alone!" she kept repeating to those around her.

„Calm down. It's me, Gina. It'll all be over in a little while. Then I'll go with you and see if the child needs help. But right now, there's no way I'll let you back out into that hell."

In the dark of the cellar, Barbara could make out the face of the young woman who had helped bring her daughter into the world. She had done so much in those first few days after the birth, when it had been so difficult for Barbara who was all alone with a newborn. Her husband was at the front in Africa and did not even know that he had a daughter.

„Oh, my poor baby! I am so afraid that Elsa with never get to meet her father! This horrid war!" sobbed Barbara on Gina's shoulder.

The sound of the departing planes had not yet died down when they ran out of the cellar. In mortal fear, Barbara raced through the bombarded city to the street where they lived. Wreckage, fire, and smoke were everywhere… a picture of complete ruin. Then, suddenly, her heart stopped beating.

There, instead of the familiar sight of her house, she saw a pile of rubble, a thin trail of smoke still rising to the gray sky above. Barbara began throwing boards and bricks right and left with her bare hands. „Elsa! Elsa, where are you? Oh Lord, please don't take my child from me!" she pleaded continually.

Gina tried to lead her away gently so that she would not get in the way of the rescue workers, who arrived soon after. But the desperate mother would not be driven away. She stepped aside only when they began to pull the dead body of a neighbor from the building next door.

„I know she's alive. Hurry, I have to feed her. It's time for her to eat," she urged the men from the rescue crew time and again.

The men looked at each other, and the expressions on their faces read, „Poor mother. She's gone crazy." They knew that only mournful discoveries awaited them.

Night was already beginning to settle again when the team of exhausted men faced the fact that they would soon have to stop. They were depressed, because they had not been able to pull anyone from the debris alive. It was not a pleasant sight, and they did not know how to get Barbara to leave the scene. One of them tried to take her gently by the shoulders, but she pulled away and cried out, „Quiet! I hear her! I can hear her crying!"

No one heard a thing, but none of the men had the strength to refuse the desperate mother help. They continued removing the debris from the place she pointed to. After only a short while, which seemed like an eternity to Barbara, they managed to lift the ceiling's cross beam. And beneath it, in a small space between the bricks – a living child! It opened its blue eyes, and its tiny, dust covered face wrinkled in spasmodic cries. Barbara rushed to her child and hurriedly unwrapped it. The baby kicked its legs and hungrily searched for its mother's breast. It had escaped completely unharmed!

„A miracle," the men shook their heads in disbelief and respectfully gave the nursing mother space. The oldest one threw a warm blanket over Barbara's shoulders and, deeply moved, made the sign of the cross on the baby's forehead.

The exhausted mother, nursing her rescued child on the pile of rubble, smiled down at it happily. „Prague Child, Holy Infant, had returned my baby to me," she whispered thankfully, and turned her eyes to the sky. Glittering flakes of first snow began to fall from the dark heavens.

The Prague Child:
A Legend Through the Ages

Long ago, a pious monk named Joseph lived in a monastery not far from the wealthy Spanish city of Seville. Protected from the outside world by the thick monastery walls, he spent his life in silent prayer and meditation. But one night the peace was disrupted when a horde of wild Moors rushed in. The heathens overran the monastery and leveled it to the ground. They killed all its inhabitants, and only Joseph and three of the other brothers were able to escape with their lives.

When the handful of monks who had survived returned to the burnt shell of the monastery, they all turned to Joseph in silent question. What to do? Should they set out for some other monastery or seek help in Seville?

Joseph decided that they will stay. Out of the ashes of the old monastery they began building a new one with their bare hands. They worked until they were exhausted: clearing the debris, erecting new walls, preparing the soil of the charred garden…

Soon though, they found themselves at the end of their strength. Their numbers could be counted on just one hand, and the work never seemed to end. Each did the work of three men. Joseph took care of the garden. From morning to night he worked, planting and watering so that they would have something to eat in the winter.

One afternoon, he sank to the earth, exhausted from his toil beneath the burning sun. He lay on the parched grass and thought to himself tiredly: „Lord, without your help, we will never build a new monastery!“ Suddenly a shadow fell across him. When he opened his eyes, a curious, childish face looked down on him.

„Who are you?“ he asked, smiling at the child.

„I am Jesus,“ said the boy, laying a hand on his hot forehead. „And I want you to know that I stand beside you.“

The monk, incapable of uttering a single word, gazed into the beautiful face of the child. He followed the direction of Jesus' gaze and, before his amazed eyes, the monastery appeared, flourishing like a garden in spring, newly built, and a hundred times more beautiful than before.

„Oh, that would be…“ he turned around. The child was gone. It had disappeared,

and the image of the renewed monastery along with it. Joseph fell to his knees in joyful prayer and, from his heart, gave thanks to the Lord…

Years passed and, with the help of God, the monastery was rebuilt to surpass even its former beauty. It looked exactly as it had appeared to Joseph during his wondrous meeting with the Son of God. The monastery flourished, but the aged Joseph, could not leave this world in peace. It was as if he still had some responsibility. Not a single day passed in which he did not think of his meeting with the Infant Jesus. That beautiful childish face kept appearing before him. He attempted to capture it on paper, carve it in wood, and model it from wax.

However, this sort of work was hard for him. His old fingers no longer wanted to obey him. As time passed by, it was harder and harder to recall that beautiful face exactly. He continually prayed for the Infant to appear to him one more time.

One day he was working in the garden and during rests he kept trying to sculpt the features of the young Christ in wax. Suddenly he heard quiet steps behind him.. He turned around and caught sight of the Child. He would have recognized him among a thousand, for He had not changed at all over the years. The Child looked at Joseph's statue and smiled kindly.

„You have come, my Lord?" the aged monk fell to his knees before him.

„I am here so that you can finish your work."

Joseph began to work the wax anew with his suddenly agile and skillful fingers. The wax softened obediently beneath his hands. By night, he had an exact copy of the Little Jesus before him, a standing figure. It was a flawless piece of work… a faithful image of that heavenly face. The face which would guide people along the path of goodness through the ages.

The child smiled in satisfaction at the sculptor, placed its small palm into Joseph's old, wrinkled hand, and together they walked away through the blooming garden, the aged monk and the heavenly child, hand in hand.

When the brothers from the monastery found Joseph's cold body in the garden with the statue of the Infant Jesus beside him, they understood at once from the joyful smile on his face how his master work had come about. They took the Holy Infant and displayed it in the cathedral. They held it in deep respect and so the monastery prospered. Spain was freed from Moorish rule, and the government was returned to the hands of the Catholic king.

The land flourished, and new monasteries sprung up everywhere. One of the founders of these magnificent constructions was the devout Carmelite sister Saint Theresa of Avila. She had the greatest respect for the Embodiment of the Holy Infant who, for the salvation of humanity, came to Earth merely as a child. She always brought an identical copy of original statuette of the Child Jesus to each newly built monastery. They dressed the original Holy Infant in splendid garments, displayed it, and carried it in ceremonial processions. People sang, danced, and rejoiced in celebration.

And how did the Holy Infant come to the Czech Lands? According to legend, Saint Theresa gave it as a gift to the pious Spanish noblewoman Isabelle Manrique de Lara. Isabelle later gave this most precious family heirloom as a wedding gift to her daughter Maria, and she brought the Holy Infant to her new home, to Prague.

Since that time, the baby Jesus belongs to the world – to all people who put their faith it him. That was the beginning of his famous legendary journey through the ages.

One day in the midst of the cruel winter of 1628, Father Ludvik, the prior of the

Carmelitan monastery in the Little Quarter, was expecting a visitor – the noble Lady Polyxena of Lobkowicz, wife of the most prominent diplomat of the Kingdom of Bohemia and daughter of the Spanish noblewoman Maria de Lara. One of the most prominent ladies of the kingdom kneeled before the prior and offered the Infant to him with these words: „I am giving you that which is the dearest to me. Hold this statue in the highest esteem and you will fare well."

At that time, mainly novitiates tended the Infant of Prague. The statue was placed in the oratory, and the young brothers prayed before it daily. After a while, they began to tell stories among themselves about a strange force that entered them from the statue, from his gaze, which saw right into their innermost being. They told the prior about this, and he then decided to display the Holy Infant in the cathedral so that other people would have access to it as well.

Soon, news of miraculous cures, unprecedented happenings, and protection from the most varied of calamities came to the brothers' ears. The Little Prague Dweller, as the city's residents began to call the statue, miraculously lent its strength to the people. It proved to be able to ease the senseless sufferings of the wars, so endless and cruel. The Holy Infant enjoyed ever greater esteem not just from the residents

of Prague. Its fame spread even beyond the borders of Prague, out into the whole Czech land.

Soon, however, hard times set on the Kingdom of Bohemia. The Saxons invaded in 1631, plundering the city without mercy. They especially liked Catholic churches and rich monasteries. The soldiers broke into the Church of Our Lady Victorious. They forced out the monks, stole what they wanted, and what remained, they destroyed. The unfortunate Holy Infant, which, in their eyes, was only a ridiculous toy, lost both arms to a soldier's sword.

When the heavy church doors banged shut as the marauders left, their rampage had not left a single stone undisturbed. The crippled Jesus Child ended up laying somewhere behind the altar. There it waited for many years for its time to come again.

The very next year the Saxons were forced out of Prague, and the Carmelites were

able to return to their monastery. But it was a miserable existence, as they were left entirely without any means. When a great plague struck Prague with another blow, death mercilessly cut down the majority of the brothers, even the prior wasn't spared. The black death did not prefer the rich or the poor – she took them all equally.

The situation became worse. Hostile armies took turns attacking Prague, and the Carmelite brothers had to flee once again – this time before the ranks of the Swedish army. Fewer and fewer people attended the Church of Our Lady Victorious. The Holy Child disappeared, and there was no one to bless the poor supplicants. There was no one to hold a protective hand in blessing over Prague.

„Dear Holy Infant, return to us," prayed the last faithful few in the devastated church. „Come and save us, as you did before."

Long after, when peace reigned once again in Prague, the Carmelites were finally able to return to their monastery again. Not one of them could guess where to look for the Prague Child. They considered it lost forever.

On All Saints' Day of 1637, Father Cyril returned to Prague to sorrowfully remember his younger years. He did not once doubt that the Prague Child was still in the monastery. Back then, he and the other novitiates in the monastery performed their devotions daily before the little Holy Infant. God's Son had given him strength, had

always helped him when things had been at their worst. Come what may, he had to find the statue. And when the Christ Child returns, things would improve again.

But he searched in vain. Even the Prior tried to convince him of the futility of his quest: „I was there myself seven years ago when those drunken soldiers pillaged the church. They destroyed whatever had no value for them. That is assuredly how the Prague Child ended up."

But then one day… Father Cyril was praying in the empty dark church. He had been kneeling for many long hours on the cold stones before the ruined, empty altar, offering prayers for the monastery. He prayed for God to take mercy on the citizens of Prague whom He trusted to Cyril's care.

Suddenly, his prayers were disturbed by the sound of a child crying. His heart was seized by this quiet lament. Puzzled, Father Cyril searched for the lost child. Then he realized that the cries were coming from behind the altar. It was as if some sort of glow emanated from there. Cautiously, he looked closer, and then his heart stopped. There, beneath the rubble shined the golden hair of the Holy Child!

„Take pity on me and I will take pity on you," he heard a sad little voice say. Father Cyril stood in shock. „Look, I have no hands. Return my arms to me, and I shall return peace to you !"

Cyril carefully unearthed the child and with the greatest tenderness, clasped it to his breast, then hurried to his cell in order to wash it clean of dust. He turned it over in his hands and, with pain, examined the tiny stumps which were all that remained of the Prague Child's arms. The statue was in complete shambles, but it was still possible to repair. But what should he do about the hands? To have them sculpted would cost a lot of money, which the monastery didn't have.

The next day, Father Cyril told the Prior of his miraculous experience. He insisted that most pressing thing now was to gather money to give the Prague Child back its arms. And then, after restoring it to its former beauty, it should be displayed in church again. But the Prior decided that there were things of more immediate importance to the monastery right now.

So the unhappy monk said to himself, „All right, I will display the statue in the church just as it is: damaged and dirty. Perhaps some good soul will take pity on it and donate the money needed for new arms."

The Holy Infant stood there sadly. It gazed down upon its humble worshipers, but it had nothing with which to bless them. One day, a veteran soldier, a Commissar, came into the church. The horrors of war had moved this man toward religion. During his life in army, which had blown him to the far corners of Europe, he had witnessed much pain and suffering. He had seen so many children affected by the horrors of war, many of them afflicted just like the Holy Infant. The images of these children continued to appear before him in his dreams. Unable to sleep at night, he often wished to die. He looked on the crippled child on the altar, with tears flowing down the gray stubble of his cheeks. He knelt in humbleness and bowed his wrinkled face to the ground. A leather pouch burned him in his pocket. It was some plunder from victorious battles. In an instant he got up, and laid the pouch before the Infant, leaving in the same silence as he had come.

Brother Cyril could not believe his eyes when he found the pouch of money at the Christ Child's feet. He hurried at once into the city to find a sculptor to create new arms. Many offered their services, for they were interested in the leather pouch. Finally he brought the one who boasted his skill the most. The sculptor knew just how to work with the soft wax – he modeled a pair of handsome arms, affixed them to the body, collected his money, and went to drink it away at the nearest tavern.

The next day, the monks prepared to serve mass. All of Prague wanted to come and see the newly repaired Prague Child. But, to their great dismay, there stood the Holy Infant on the altar, armless once again!

Father Cyril thought that this simply called for someone with greater skill, and so he brought in a well known artist to repair the faulty work. This man modeled new arms, fastened them carefully to the body, and tested them several times to make sure that they would hold. Everything seemed fine, and so he took his payment and left.

The next morning, however, a sorrowful Father Cyril found the arms once again on the floor. He wracked his brains as to what he could possibly be doing wrong. He called in one artist after another. He tried having the wax arms covered in wood so that they would hold better, but it was all in vain. The arms fell off every time.

Once, however, a shy young man came to the monastery, and he offered that he will try to repair the sculpture. No one knew who he was. He was certainly not from Prague, and perhaps he was not even a sculptor. He seemed far too young to Father Cyril to manage such a task, which was too difficult even for the greatest artists. But he finally agreed to let him try, but he would not let him out from under his eyes.

Much to his surprise, the young man did not at all behave like a sculptor working with materials. He handled the Holy Infant as if it were a sick child. How gently he touched the sculpture! He took the crippled little body into his arms and, for a long

time, carefully examined him much like a doctor would. Then he tenderly made slight adjustments to the arms, affixing them so delicately that the brothers were afraid they would not hold this time either. He worked late into the night, and when he had at last finished, he soothed the Christ Child a while longer in his arms.

Those in the monastery were not able to sleep that night. At dawn, everyone rushed into the cathedral. The first rays of the morning sun lit the dark altar, and there shone the satisfied face of the Prague Infant, this time with both arms! At last the Holy Infant had been restored to health. Its right hand was raised in blessing over the monks as they arrived, kneeled and gave thanks to God.

When the monks wished to pay the young artist for his services, they could not find him anywhere . It was as if he had been swallowed up by the ground. No one knew a thing about him. Who was he? Everyone in Prague asked this question, and they looked for him all over the city. But it was all in vain. He was not an ordinary human, ran the whispers. He must be an angel who was sent from heaven to heal the Child which had been so cruelly mishandled.

The legend of the mysterious sculptor spread across the city's borders, and the curious crowds began visiting again the Church of Our Lady. And the Prague Child again enjoyed the highest respect from the city's inhabitants. When it saved the city at the time of the Swedish siege, the people's gratitude showed no bounds.

One day, a pale, tired-looking man sought out Father Cyril. It was the Duke of Kolowrat, who was among the richest noblemen in the kingdom. Desperate and nearly without hope, he had come to beg the Prague Child to help his much beloved

wife, the Duchess Elisabeth. She had been seriously ill for some time. A mysterious disease had robbed her of her sight and hearing, and the doctors had given up all hope. The desperate Duke would have done anything for his wife, regardless of the costs. He had not given up on her; he kept inviting the most famous doctors from all of Europe, but the Elisabeth kept getting worse.

Father Cyril could not refuse the unfortunate man. Furthermore, the Duchess Elisabeth was the cousin of Polyxena of Lobkowicz, who had bestowed the Prague Child on the monastery eleven years before. He fetched the precious statue and hurried to the dying woman's bedside.

When he entered her darkened chamber, Father Cyril gently placed the Prague Child in her arms. The pious woman trembled, whispering, „Oh, the Prague Child is here, here in my palace…" She kissed the Holy Child on its face and clasped it to her breast. Father Cyril kneeled beside her bed in silent prayer.

After a time, the ill woman slowly opened her eyes and, in a weak voice, cried out in wonder: „Oh! Lord, I see him! I see the Prague Child! I can see you all!" Soon after, she attempted getting out of bed, and even her hearing miraculously returned. She improved daily and could soon leave the house. Once, she ordered that her carriage be harnessed, because she wanted to make a trip outside of Prague. She seated herself in the carriage and the driver cracked his whip, but the carriage remained standing in its place. Even though six strong horses strained at the harness, the carriage would not move even an inch.

The trembling Duchess got out of the carriage, and she understood what had happened. How could she have been so selfish! She had already regained her health long ago, yet the Prague Child was still in her possession And so, with great humbleness, she set out to return the miraculous statue to Father Cyril. This time, the carriage flew like the wind.

Stories about the favors bestowed upon the Prague Child by the rich and powerful did not, unfortunately, escape the greedy ears of unbelievers. One thief could not resist such a temptation and so decided to steal from the Prague Child. He waited

patiently, hiding himself in the dark church, until the last of the believers had finished their prayers and the heavy gate had closed behind them. Then, his time had come. On tip toes he approached the Christ Child. The glitter of the eternal light of the crown on its head, inset with precious stones, lured him onward.

He gathered his courage and took two steps forward. All he had to do was reach out a hand and… suddenly he stopped and his feet became grounded. „You dare to steal from Jesus," a clear, childish voice called, petrifying him with its words. And the thief remained standing there the whole night long like a statue incapable of motion, hand outstretched, until morning came and Father Cyril arrived to release him from his torment. The good father let the man go. Everyone was surprised, but he said to them, „He will steal no more. And word of this will spread, so that all will know what will happen to those who wish to steal from the Prague Child."

The Infant of Prague's fame spread even further throughout the world. Pilgrims from all different lands came to the altar to bow to him like to a true king. In the year 1651, a great celebration was held in Prague, in which the Prague Child officially received the title of „Merciful." It was carried from church to church in splendid procession and even received a gold crown from one of its great admirers, the Duke of Martinic.

Four years later, an even greater celebration took place. The Archbishop of Prague crowned the Prague Child with a magnificent headpiece set with pearls and precious stones, and bestowed the Order of the Golden Fleece upon the holy statue. Divine services are still conducted to this day on the anniversary of the Assumption of the Lord in commemoration of that splenderous coronation.

The Prague Child was placed into a crystal cabinet in the exquisitely decorated chapel of the Church of Our Lady Victorious. In time, the chapel was not sufficient for the amount of visitors, and the statue was then moved to the center of the

cathedral. It still stands there today: on the side altar in a magnificent glass cabinet made of fine-worked silver. Empress Marie Theresa, also a great admirer of the Prague Child, was one among the vast array of other notable personages who sought its assistance. Her gift of exquisite garments are, to this day, among the most precious in the Prague Child's wardrobe.

In the year 1741, the armies of the Bavarian Prince Karel Albert invaded Prague, and he crowned himself the King of Bohemia. Fortunately, under his rule, Prague did not suffer any great harm, and the grateful inhabitants attributed this to the Prague Child's protective presence.

Same thing took place three years later during the Prussian attacks. At that time, the Prague Child was carried through the city in a procession as people begged for salvation of Prague from the destructive force of the Prussian army. And that is exactly what happened – the Prussians pulled out without spilling a drop of blood, and the grateful inhabitants of Prague gave the Christ Child many gifts and showed it much love.

In the year 1784, during the rule of Joseph II, the Carmelite monastery was destroyed. Hard times again befell the Prague Child. It was entrusted to the care of the Order of the Knights of Maltese, and it received neither money nor even the most basic of repairs to its altar. Because of this, it was necessary to „go begging" from church to church in Prague. There it was on display until the funds necessary for the repair of the Church of Our Lady Victorious were raised.

But even though no one in Prague watched over the Child carefully at that time, its fame grew rapidly in the rest of the world. Word of it had penetrated mainly to Spain, the land of its origin, and into Italy, where the Carmelite Monastery in Arenzano offered prayer in its honor. Further, it was also known in France, Great Britain, and Holland. Later it even made its way to the United States, India, the Phillippines, China, and Vietnam. Churches dedicated to the Prague Child grew up all over the world, and in each one was a carefully made copy of the statue. Prayers, gifts, and letters of thanks continued to arrive in Prague from everywhere.

In 1993, the Archbishop of Prague invited two young monks from Arenzano, Italy,

to the monastery, which had been newly restored. Their task was to care for the Prague Child and to show it the respect it rightfully deserved. Thus, the Barefooted Carmelites returned again to their monastery in the Little Quarter which was always the only home of the Prague Infant.

Today, as in Baroque times, pilgrims from all corners of the earth come to visit the cathedral. For generations, people have been kneeling and praying before the gracious face of the "Little Praguer", begging mercy for themselves and their loved ones. The Infant Jesus never let anyone with a sincere heart leave empty-handed. For it was He who preached: „Honor me and I shall protect you."

To be published in the series THE LEGENDS OF PRAGUE:

The Legend of Golem

The Legend of the Astronomical Clock of the Old Town

The Legend of the Charles Bridge

The Legend of the Loreta Bells

The Legend
OF THE INFANT
OF PRAGUE

Published in Czech Republic by MEANDER Publishing house,
Zubatého 1, 150 00 Praha 5
e-mail: meander@volny.cz, www.meander.cz
© Ivana Pecháčková
Translation: Miriam Fitting
Cover design: Jarmila Marešová
Illustrations: Jarmila Marešová
Graphic design and technical editor: Jaroslava Harantová
Editorial staff: Koren Riesterer, Klára Tvarůžková
Typeset by MU Typografické Studio, Rumunská 26, Praha 2
Bound by ČTK repro a. s. Praha
Printed in the Czech Republic by Ekon družstvo, Srázná 17, Jihlava
Second edition
ISBN: 80-902373-6-3